This book belongs to

_____

DISNEP

The

JungleBook

The Story of Mowgli

Disney

The Jungle Book

The Story of Mowgli

Bath • New York • Cologne • Melbourne • Delhi
Hong Kong • Shenzhen • Singapore

This edition published by Parragon Books Ltd in 2016
and distributed by

Parragon Inc.
440 Park Avenue South, 13th Floor
New York, NY 10016
www.parragon.com

ISBN 978-1-4748-5039-1

Printed in China

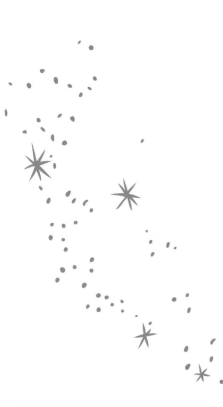

*Forget about your
worries and your strife!*

Long ago, deep in the jungles of India, there lived a wise and kind panther named Bagheera. One day, as Bagheera walked along the river, he saw something surprising—a baby! The baby was lying in a boat that had crashed onto the shore. "Why, it's a Man-cub!" the panther said to himself.

The Man-cub was in urgent need of food and care, but the closest Man-village was days away. So, Bagheera took the baby to a nearby wolf family. The mother had just had pups, and Bagheera hoped she would accept the Man-cub as one of her own.

The panther placed the baby near the den and stepped away.
After a few quick sniffs, the mother wolf gently carried the
baby into her den. Bagheera's plan had worked!

For the next 10 years, Mowgli, as the Man-cub came to be called, lived happily with the wolves. He quickly became a favorite among all the jungle animals. All, that is, except Shere Khan, a strong and cunning tiger.

Shere Khan feared only
Man's gun and Man's fire. He
had heard of the young Man-cub
and believed that Mowgli would
grow up to be a hunter. The tiger
wanted to make sure that
didn't happen.

One night, the wolves met at Council Rock to discuss the matter. Akela, the wolf leader, declared that, for everyone's safety, Mowgli would have to leave the pack.

"But the boy cannot survive alone in the jungle!" protested Mowgli's wolf father, Rama.

Bagheera had been listening to the wolves. He jumped down from his perch in the tree and approached Akela and Rama.

"Maybe I can help," he said. "I know a Man-village where Mowgli would be safe. I can take him there."

"So be it," said Akela. "There is no time to lose. Good luck!"

And so, early the next morning, Bagheera and Mowgli set out. They traveled well into the night and were soon deep in the jungle.

"Bagheera," said Mowgli, "I'm getting sleepy. Shouldn't we start back home?"

Bagheera told Mowgli about Shere Khan and the wolf council's decision. Mowgli was shocked.

"I don't want to go to the Man-village!" he protested.

Bagheera promised
Mowgli that things
would seem better in the
morning. He helped the
Man-cub climb a tall tree.
"We'll be safer up here," the panther said.
    They settled down on a tree branch,
and in no time at all Bagheera was
sound asleep, while Mowgli brooded over
his fate. Neither one noticed Kaa, the
snake, slithering toward Mowgli.

"Ssssay now, what have we here?" said Kaa.

"It's a Man-cub. A delicious Man-cub."

Mowgli tried to shove Kaa out of his face. "Oh, go away and leave me alone," he said, annoyed.

Kaa refused to leave. He kept slithering toward Mowgli, and when Mowgli finally looked straight at Kaa, the snake used his eyes to put Mowgli into a trance.

Kaa coiled himself around
Mowgli and was preparing to eat
him! Suddenly, Bagheera woke up
and saw what was happening.

Moving quickly, the panther
slapped Kaa on the head. The snake
released Mowgli from his grip.

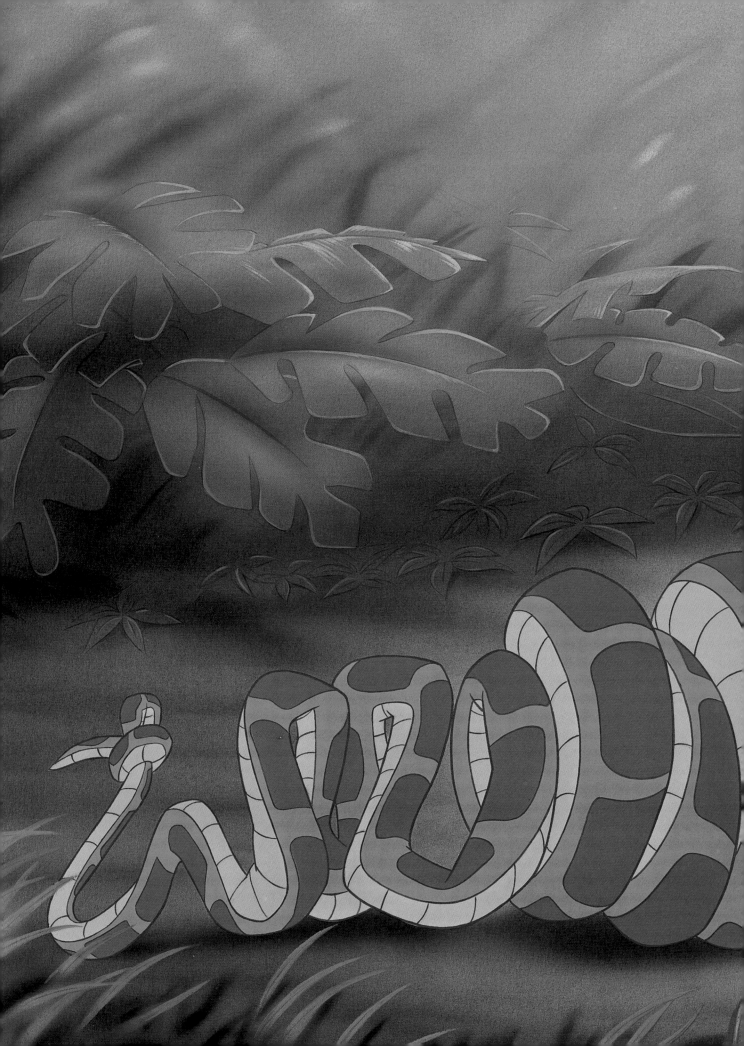

An angry Kaa turned on Bagheera.
However, before the snake could coil himself
around Bagheera, Mowgli pushed him off
the tree branch. A defeated and hungry Kaa
slithered off.

The next morning, Mowgli and
Bagheera were awakened by a loud
rumbling and shaking.

"A parade!" Mowgli shouted
enthusiastically.

Bagheera covered his ears and groaned,
"Oh no, the dawn patrol again!"

Mowgli grabbed a vine and swung
down from the tree to take a look.

Mowgli watched as a long line of elephants marched proudly along in single file. He hurried over to a baby elephant at the very end of the line.

"Can I join in?" asked Mowgli.

"Sure!" said the baby elephant. "Just do what I do!"

Mowgli got in step behind the baby elephant and began to march along. It was a lot of fun. Then he got down on all fours to walk more like the elephants in front of him.

Suddenly, Colonel Hathi, the elephant at the head of the line, called out, "To the rear, march!"

Mowgli did not know that meant the entire company had to turn around. He and the baby elephant bumped into each other.

"Company, halt!" Colonel Hathi shouted, and all the elephants stopped and stood ready for inspection. Mowgli tried to fit in, but Colonel Hathi figured out that Mowgli was a Man-cub.

The Colonel lifted Mowgli high
with his trunk. "I'll have no Man-cub
in my jungle!" he cried.
At that moment, Bagheera rushed over.
"The Man-cub is with me," he told Colonel
Hathi. "I'm taking him to the Man-village."
"Good!" said the elephant. "And remember, an elephant
never forgets!" With that, Colonel Hathi turned and
marched off with his troop.

"You're going to the Man-village right now!" said Bagheera.

"I'm staying right here!" Mowgli cried. He wrapped his arms around a small tree.

"You're going if I have to drag you!" shouted Bagheera, and he tried, unsuccessfully, to pull Mowgli off the tree.

Bagheera lost his temper. "From now on, you're on your own!" he declared and stalked off.

"Don't worry about me!" an equally angry Mowgli yelled after him.

Mowgli wandered through the jungle and finally came to rest against a large rock. He heard rustling leaves, and suddenly a bear named Baloo appeared.

Mowgli was upset after his fight with Bagheera, but once Baloo arrived, it was hard to stay in a bad mood!

Baloo offered to teach Mowgli about the bare necessities of life in the jungle. He showed Mowgli how to find bananas, coconuts, and other foods. He showed him how to scratch his back on a tree, too. The whole time Baloo sang and danced. Mowgli couldn't help but smile and feel better.

The two new friends splashed and played in the river and then floated contentedly downstream together. Mowgli joined in as Baloo sang some more.

"I like being a bear!" said Mowgli.

"You're going to make one swell bear!" said Baloo. "Why, you even sing like one!"

Suddenly, a group of monkeys
swooped down from the trees and
grabbed Mowgli!

"Hey!" screamed Mowgli. "Let go
of me!"

He struggled against the monkeys, but
they just laughed and held onto him.

Baloo angrily shook his fist at the monkeys and demanded that they release Mowgli.

"Come on and get him!" taunted one of the monkeys.

The monkeys aimed a steady chorus of jeers and insults at Baloo. They aimed plenty of fruit at him, too!

The monkeys swung through the trees, tossing Mowgli along as they went. "Baloo!" cried Mowgli. "Help me! They're carrying me away."

Baloo knew he needed Bagheera to help him. He called for the panther as loudly as he could. As soon as Bagheera heard Baloo's cries, he hurried toward the bear.

Baloo told Bagheera that the monkeys had carried Mowgli off.

Bagheera suspected that the monkeys were taking Mowgli to the ruins of an ancient city where their ruler, an orangutan named King Louie, lived.

Bagheera and Baloo set off at once to save Mowgli.

Meanwhile, as King Louie and the monkeys danced and sang, the king told Mowgli that he dreamed of being human. He had heard that Mowgli wanted to stay in the jungle, and he offered to help the Man-cub. In return, the king wanted Mowgli to tell him the secret of how people made fire.

"But, I don't know how to make fire," Mowgli said. King Louie didn't believe him.

Bagheera and Baloo arrived at the ruins in
time to hear what King Louie wanted.
Bagheera quickly came up with a plan.
"While you create a disturbance," he said to
Baloo, "I'll rescue Mowgli."

Baloo disguised himself as an ape and burst in to join the dancing. King Louie took one look at the newcomer and began to dance with him!

Bagheera tried to grab Mowgli,
but every time he got close, one
of the monkeys would whirl the
boy away from him. Meanwhile,
Baloo continued to dance with
King Louie, who didn't suspect
a thing.

But Baloo was enjoying himself so much that he didn't notice when his disguise started to slip. King Louie was furious that he'd been tricked! He and the other monkeys began to chase Baloo and Bagheera.

But Baloo wasn't leaving without the Man-cub!
He grabbed Mowgli and tried to pull him out of
King Louie's grasp. King Louie grabbed a pillar, and
the whole thing came crashing down—giving poor
Baloo a black eye!

By the time Baloo and
Bagheera were finally able to
get Mowgli away from King
Louie and the monkeys, the
ancient ruins had crumbled
around the king and his
monkey court!

That night, while Mowgli slept,
Bagheera explained to Baloo that
Shere Khan was after the Man-cub.
He convinced Baloo that Mowgli
was not safe in the jungle.

The next morning, Baloo
reluctantly told Mowgli,
"I've got to take you to
the Man-village."

Hurt and disappointed, Mowgli ran
away. Baloo tried to follow him, but the
Man-cub was too fast, and soon left Baloo
behind. Baloo ran to tell Bagheera. They had
to find Mowgli before something terrible
happened to him!

Shere Khan was hunting in the jungle when he overheard Bagheera talking to Colonel Hathi.

"I need your help," Bagheera said. "The Man-cub must be found."

Shere Khan knew then that the Man-cub was alone. He began prowling through the jungle looking for Mowgli.

As Mowgli wandered through the jungle, he met Kaa again. Kaa tricked Mowgli into thinking he could be trusted and then hypnotized him, wrapping him up tight in his coils. He didn't want the Man-cub to escape this time!

Shere Khan was passing by when he heard Kaa singing. He called the snake down and said he wanted a word with him.

"I thought perhaps you were entertaining someone up there in your coils," the tiger said. "You were singing to someone. Who is it, Kaa?"

Kaa didn't want to share the Man-cub, so he told Shere Khan he was singing to himself. Kaa tried to hypnotize the tiger, but it didn't work.

While Shere Khan and Kaa were talking, Mowgli woke up and managed to escape from the snake's coils. He ran off into the jungle once more, feeling more alone than ever before.

Mowgli arrived at a place in the jungle where there was very little grass on the ground and the trees were bare. He was soon joined by four vultures.

At first, the vultures tried to tease Mowgli. "He's got legs like a stork," one vulture said.

"But he doesn't have any feathers," said another. All the vultures laughed until they saw how sad Mowgli was. They sang a friendship song to him to cheer him up. Mowgli began to smile, and soon he was clapping along.

Shere Khan overheard the singing and found Mowgli and the vultures.

"Bravo! Bravo!" he said to the vultures when they finished their song. "And thank you for detaining my victim."

The vultures were frightened and flew off. From the safety of a tree, they urged Mowgli to run.

But Mowgli turned to Shere Khan and said, "You don't scare me."

Mowgli refused to run from the tiger. Shere Khan counted to 10 and then leaped at Mowgli with all his claws out and his mouth wide open!

Baloo arrived in the nick of time and pulled Shere Khan's tail so hard, the tiger missed the Man-cub. The vultures grabbed Mowgli while Baloo held Shere Khan off. But the tiger was strong, and he soon managed to get free.

As the vultures carried Mowgli to safety, a storm
began. Lightning struck the branches of a dead tree,
setting it on fire. This gave Mowgli an idea.

Mowgli knew that fire was one of the only things that Shere Khan feared. He grabbed a burning branch from the dead tree and bravely ran to where Shere Khan was fighting Baloo.

Mowgli tied the burning branch to Shere Khan's tail. The tiger leapt and yowled in fright. He ran as fast as he could into the jungle, never to be seen again.

But Baloo was badly injured. He lay on the
ground, his eyes closed.

"Baloo, please get up," Mowgli said sadly.
He hugged his friend.

Finally, Baloo opened his eyes and lifted his head. He was okay. Overjoyed, Mowgli ran and sprang into the bear's arms.

Baloo, Bagheera, and Mowgli
set off once again, and at long last,
they reached the Man-village.

Mowgli climbed a tree to get a good look at
a beautiful girl he heard singing by a watering
hole. To Bagheera's great delight, he couldn't
take his eyes off her.

When the girl saw Mowgli, she smiled shyly
at him.

The girl dropped her jug, and it rolled to Mowgli's feet. He picked it up and followed the girl to the Man-village. He turned around to give Baloo and Bagheera a big, goofy grin.

"Mowgli is where he belongs now," said Bagheera.

"I think you're right," said Baloo, and he and Bagheera danced happily back into the jungle.

The End